READING

RECOVERY

Weekly Reader Books presents

PIET POTTER'S FIRST CASE

Story and Pictures by
ROBERT QUACKENBUSH

A Piet Potter Mystery

McGRAW-HILL BOOK COMPANY

NEW YORK • St. Louis • San Francisco
Düsseldorf • London • Mexico • Sydney • Toronto

This book is a presentation of
Weekly Reader Books.

Weekly Reader Books offers
book clubs for children from
preschool through junior high school.
All quality hardcover books are selected by
a distinguished Weekly Reader Selection Board.

For further information write to:
Weekly Reader Books
1250 Fairwood Ave.
Columbus, Ohio 43216

Library of Congress Cataloging in Publication Data

Quackenbush, Robert M
    Piet Potter's first case.

    (A Piet Potter mystery ; 1)
    SUMMARY: A boy detective uses a blank sheet of
paper, a key, and a subway map to help a neighbor solve
a puzzling message in a will.
    [1. Mystery and detective stories] I. Title.
PZ7.Q16Pi   [E]   79-21258
ISBN 0-07-051021-0

FOR PIET

and young mystery fans

everywhere

The apartment house
on East 77th Street
buzzed with excitement.
Someone famous had just
moved into the building.
It was Piet Potter,
the amazing boy private eye.

Piet (it rhymes with neat)
and his parents
took an apartment
on the fourteenth floor.

Mr. and Mrs. Benton
in apartment 3B
gave Piet his first case.
They called and asked
for his help.

Piet went to see them.

"What is the problem?"
he asked.

Mr. Benton pointed
to an old desk.
He said, "Our rich
Uncle Henry passed away
and left us this desk
and a million dollars
if we can find it."

Mrs. Benton said,
"But the money
is not in the desk.
It is hidden somewhere.
We must find it
before morning."

"If we don't,"
Mr. Benton said,
"the money and the desk
will go to Uncle Henry's
lawyer, Mr. Jacobs.
Only Mr. Jacobs knows
where the money is hidden."

"Uncle Henry made
his fortune overnight,"
said Mrs. Benton.
"I guess he wanted to see
if we were smart enough
to do the same thing.
Can you help us
find the money?"

"Glad to," said Piet.
"Were there any clues
that might tell us where
the money is hidden?"

Mr. Benton opened
a drawer on the desk
and pulled out
a folded sheet of paper.
He handed it to Piet.

"None, unless you call
this a clue," he said.
"It is the only thing
in the desk."

Piet unfolded the paper.

"But this sheet of paper
has nothing on it," he said.

"We know," said Mr. Benton.

Piet took the paper
and held it under a lamp.
He examined it
with his magnifying glass.
(He never overlooked a clue.)

"Well, well," he said
at last. "It so happens
that this paper
is not blank, after all."

"How can that be?"
asked Mr. Benton.

Piet answered,
"I'll show you.
Please bring me some ink
and a small brush."

Mrs. Benton got
the ink and the brush.

Piet dipped the brush
into the bottle of ink
and painted the paper.

"Why, there is a message
written on the paper!"
cried Mrs. Benton.
"How did you know that?"
Piet answered, "I saw
flakes of white wax crayon
on the paper
with my magnifying glass.
So I painted the paper
with ink because
ink and wax don't mix.
That made it possible
for us to read
the secret message."

"What does the message say?"
asked Mr. Benton eagerly.

Piet answered, "It says
to turn a knob on the
upper right-hand drawer
of the desk.
It also gives numbers
for the lock of a safe."

"Amazing!" said Mrs. Benton.

"That's my middle name,"
said Piet.

Mr. Benton went over
and turned the knob
on the proper drawer.
At once, a panel on the desk
slid back, revealing a safe.

"Look!" cried Mrs. Benton.

"Please read the
safe's numbers so I can
open it," said Mr. Benton.

Piet read, "Two right,
four left, and thirty right."

Mr. Benton turned
the knob on the safe.
Suddenly, the safe door
clicked open!

Quickly, Mr. Benton
reached into the safe
and felt around.

"There is no money
in the safe!" he cried.
"Only an envelope!"

"Open it, dear,"
said Mrs. Benton.
"There might be a check
for the money
inside the envelope."
Mr. Benton opened
the envelope.
"Sorry, no check,"
he said. "There's just
a letter, a key,
and a subway map."
"Oh, no," said Mrs. Benton.
Piet stepped forward.
He said, "May I have
a look at those things?"

Mr. Benton handed over

the letter, the key, and the map.

Piet read the letter aloud:

"Dear Mary,

Timothy misses you already.

Your Bo-Bo misses you, too.

And so does little Marilyn.

You forgot to take along an

extra key for the cupboard.

I have slipped it in for you.

Love,

Uncle Henry"

Piet finished reading.

"The letter makes no sense,"

said Mr. Benton.

"I don't think it is
supposed to make sense,"
said Piet, as he
kept shifting the letter
across the subway map.
Then he stopped.

"Well, well," he said.
"I believe I know where
your money is hidden.
Shall we take a taxi
or the subway?"

"A taxi," said the Bentons.

They all went downstairs
to hail a taxi.

"Grand Central Terminal,"
Piet said to the driver.

The taxi sped away.

When the taxi
pulled up at Grand Central,
Piet and the Bentons
hopped out and ran
through the terminal.
They kept on running
until they came to
a row of steel lockers
for storing suitcases.

Piet looked
at locker numbers
until he found a locker
with the same numbers
as the key from the safe.
Then he opened the locker
with the key.

"Look! A suitcase!"
Mrs. Benton cried to Piet.
"It must contain the money.
How did you know
it would be here?"

"Easy," answered Piet,
as he held the letter
next to the subway map.
"Notice the periods
in the letter.
They fit the
five subway stops
from where we live
to Grand Central.
The locker key
filled in the rest."

"Amazing," said Mr. Benton.

"It's his middle name,"
said Mrs. Benton.

Piet opened the suitcase.
There was no money inside.
It was filled with
hundreds of chopsticks!

"Oh, no!" moaned Mrs. Benton.
"Now what?"

"Be patient," said Piet.
"I think this is just
another clue to show us
where the money
is really hidden."

He dug around
among the chopsticks
and pulled out
two big spice shakers
and a plastic chip stamped
with the number 44.

Mr. Benton said,
"I know what this is about.
That plastic numbered chip
is given out where people
check their coats.
The chopsticks must mean
that the money is hidden
in a checkroom
in a Chinese restaurant.
But which one?
There are hundreds."

"Good thinking,
Mr. Benton," said Piet.
"But I don't think it is
a Chinese restaurant
we should be looking for.
Wait here, while I go
look up an address."

Piet ran to the
nearest phone booth
and looked up an address
in the yellow pages.
Then he came running back.
"Follow me," he said.

They all ran outside
to the street.
They ran a few blocks
until they came to
a restaurant.

"Are you sure this
is the right place?"
asked Mr. Benton.

"Quite sure," said Piet.
"Everything in the suitcase
is about this place."

"But this is a
Japanese restaurant,"
said Mr. and Mrs. Benton.
"Do people eat with
chopsticks here?"

"Yes," said Piet.

"And there is more.

The shakers I found

in the suitcase

are the same kind

that I've seen used

by the chefs at

restaurants of this type.

They toss the shakers

up in the air for show

as they cook at your table.

Cooking at the table

is often featured at

Japanese restaurants—not at

Chinese restaurants."

"But what about the

numbered chip?"

asked Mr. Benton.

Piet answered,
"It's from the
checkroom inside.
It has the same number
as the street where
this restaurant is located
—44th Street."

Mr. Benton started
to say "amazing" again.
But he stopped himself.

They all went
into the restaurant.
They stopped at
the checkroom.
Mr. Benton handed
the numbered chip
to the hat-check woman.

"Oh," she said.

"I've been expecting you.
Are you Mr. Benton?"

Mr. Benton nodded.

The hat-check woman
reached under the counter
and handed Mr. Benton
an envelope.

"Will you be staying
for dinner?" she asked.

Mr. Benton opened
the envelope.
Inside was a check
for one million dollars.

"Yes, we will be staying
for dinner!" he said.

And they all stayed
and had a big celebration.
Thanks to Piet Potter's
smooth sleuthing
which was, as always,
AMAZING.

ABOUT THE AUTHOR

Robert Quackenbush is the author
and illustrator of many books for
children, including several popular
mysteries. A native of Arizona,
he now lives in New York City
with his wife and young son, Piet,
who loves the city for its playgrounds
and activities, and who is the inspiration
for this exciting new mystery series.

Other Piet Potter mysteries:

PIET POTTER RETURNS